Copyright © 2003 by Nord-Süd Verlag AG, Gossau Zürich, Switzerland.
First published in Switzerland under the title *Fuchs und Storch*.
English translation copyright © 2003 by North-South Books Inc., New York

First published in the United States, Great Britain, Canada, Australia,
and New Zealand in 2003 by North-South Books, an imprint
of Nord-Süd Verlag AG, Gossau Zürich, Switzerland.

Distributed in the United States by North-South Books Inc., New York.

Library of Congress Cataloging-in-Publication Data is available.
A CIP catalogue record for this book is available from The British Library.
ISBN 0-7358-1809-6 (trade edition)
1 3 5 7 9 HC 10 8 6 4 2
ISBN 0-7358-1810-X (library edition)
1 3 5 7 9 LE 10 8 6 4 2

PRINTED IN SWITZERLAND

For more information about our books, and the authors and artists
who create them, visit our web site: www.northsouth.com

THE FOX AND THE STORK

A FABLE BY AESOP

RETOLD BY **KARL RÜHMANN**

ILLUSTRATED BY **ALESSANDRA ROBERTI**

TRANSLATED BY ANTHEA BELL

NORTH-SOUTH BOOKS

NEW YORK / LONDON

Belongs: (— —) Name

ONE fine summer morning Stork looked out over the edge of her nest. Her tummy was rumbling. She had to find something to eat, and fast!

Fox was sitting outside his den at the edge of the woods, happily sunning himself. He'd had good hunting the night before, and now he was simmering a pan of soup over his fire.

"Good morning, Fox," said Stork, as she touched down next to him. "Oh, what a lovely smell! Is that your lunch?"

"It certainly is!" replied Fox. "Delicious mouse-tail soup!"

Stork's mouth was watering. Mouse-tail soup! It sounded very tempting. Stork had never tasted anything like that!

Of course Fox knew at once that Stork wanted some of his soup. Fox was sly and cunning, and he liked to play tricks. So he bowed and said, "May I invite you to lunch with me later today?"

"Oh yes, I'd love to come! Thank you very much," said Stork happily. "When shall I arrive?"

"Well, the soup will be ready at about twelve o'clock," said Fox. "I'll have had time to prepare for your visit by then."

"I'll be there on the dot!" promised Stork, rising
in the air again and flying away. Cunning Fox grinned
as he watched her go.

Oh yes, he'd get everything ready and no mistake!

Stork flew straight back to her nest. Her tummy was still rumbling, but she wasn't planning to spoil her appetite for lunch. Who'd want to bother catching toads when there would soon be mouse-tail soup on the menu?

Stork prettied herself up. She groomed and cleaned her feathers until they shone. Then she looked for a present for Fox.

Meanwhile Fox was strolling through the woods. He pulled up a couple of wild carrots. They'll make the mouse-tail soup taste even better, he thought. And he picked some small, sweet blueberries for dessert. Mmm, they'd taste wonderful! Then he hurried back to his den. There was still a lot to do!

Stork knocked on Fox's door at noon. She had brought Fox a bunch of flowers from her garden. "Thank you for inviting me!" she said politely, and her tummy rumbled again.

"Come along in and sit down," said Fox, grinning. "I've already set the table."

Expectantly, Stork sat down.

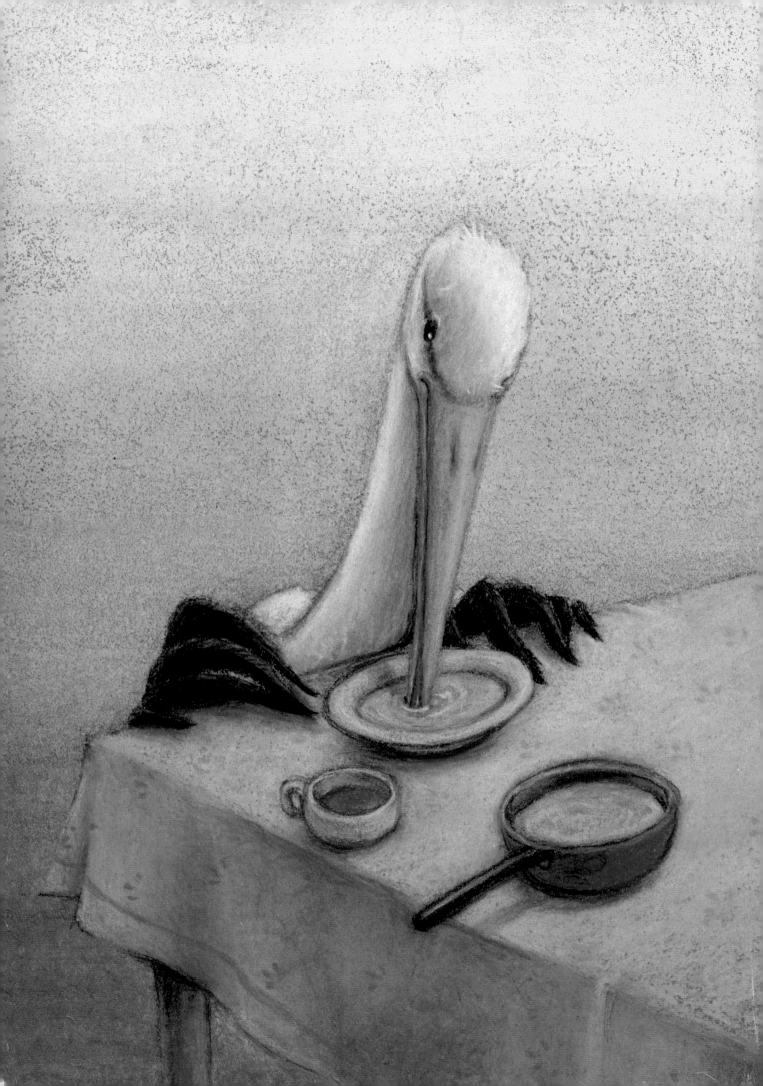

Then Fox brought in the soup—the delicious mouse-tail soup that smelled so good. But poor Stork couldn't drink any of it. When she dipped her sharp beak into the shallow plate she could stir the soup around, but only a few drops clung to her beak.

"Dear me, you've hardly touched it," said Fox.
"Still, it would be a shame to throw such good soup
away." Smacking his lips with satisfaction, he started
in on Stork's helping—just as he'd been planning to
do all along.

Stork watched him with wide eyes. Fox's mean
trick left her speechless.

But then she had a cunning idea of her own.

"That was simply delicious, dear Fox!" said Stork in a friendly voice. "Would you like to come to dinner with me tomorrow? I'll make you something really special—tender frogs stewed with wild herbs."

My, that sounds good, thought the greedy fox. "Oh yes, I'd be happy to come. Thank you very much!" he said.

As soon as he was alone again Fox started laughing. Silly Stork hadn't even noticed the way he'd tricked her!

The next day, all spruced up, Fox went over to Stork's place. He handed her a flower he had stolen from her garden.

"Come on in, dear Fox!" smiled Stork. "Dinner's ready!"

Fox could smell it. His mouth was watering with greed.

Stork served up the frog stew in tall, long-necked jars.
She easily dipped her long beak into the narrow opening
of her jar, but Fox couldn't get his nose past the opening.

"Don't you like your dinner?" asked Stork anxiously.
"Well, it would be a shame to throw this good stew away!"

So poor Fox had to sit and watch all his delicious tidbits
disappear in Stork's beak.

This time it was Fox who slunk away with his
tummy rumbling, and Stork who had the last laugh!